This book
belongs to:

_____

MESSAGE TO PARENTS

This book is perfect for parents and children to read aloud together. First read the story to your child. When you read it again, run your finger under each line, stopping at each picture for your child to "read." Help your child to figure out the picture. If your child makes a mistake, be encouraging as you say the right word. Point out the written word beneath each picture in the margin on the page. Soon your child will be "reading" aloud with you, and at the same time learning the symbols that stand for words.

Library of Congress Cataloging-in-Publication Data

Dubowski, Cathy East.
  The story of Epaminondas / retold by Cathy Dubowski ; illustrated by Mark Dubowski.
    p. cm. — (A Read along with me book)
  Summary: In attempting to follow his mother's instructions, a little boy always does the right thing at the wrong time, in this story told in rebus format.
  ISBN 0-02-898240-1
  [1. Humorous stories. 2. Rebuses.] I. Dubowski, Mark, ill.
II. Title. III. Series.
PZ7.D8544St 1989
[E]—dc19

                                        89-587
                                        CIP
                                        AC

The Story of Epaminondas

A Read Along With Me Book

Retold by **Cathy Dubowski**
Illustrated by **Mark Dubowski**

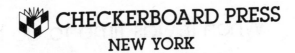

CHECKERBOARD PRESS
NEW YORK

boy

May

Once there was a good little

named Epaminondas. He loved to

visit his Auntie  and his Auntie

 loved to have him visit.

When it was time to go home,

Auntie  always gave him

something good to take with him.

One day Auntie  gave

Epaminondas a big piece of  .

"Now, hold this  tightly so

you won't drop it," she said.

cake

May

road

house

cake

hands

boy

"Yes, Auntie ," said

Epaminondas. Then he hurried

down the to his .

Epaminondas held the in his

 as tightly as he could. For

he was a good little and he

always did EXACTLY as he was told.

But Epaminondas held the
too tightly. When he got home, all

he had in his  were  !

"Oh, dear," said his  . "That is

no way to carry  ! Next time

wrap it and put it under your  .

Then carry it home."

"Yes,  ," said Epaminondas.

"I won't forget."

sun

May

butter

The next day, as soon as the

came up, Epaminondas ran to visit

his Auntie again.

When it was time to go home

his Auntie gave him some

sweet homemade .

Epaminondas remembered what

his  had told him. So he

wrapped up the sweet ,

put it under his , and hurried

down the to his .

For he was a good little and

he always did EXACTLY as he was told.

That day the  sun was very hot.

By the time Epaminondas got

home, the butter had melted.

"Oh, dear," said his Mama . "That is

no way to carry butter ! Next time

wrap it in some leaves and stop

now and then to cool it in the river

that runs along the road to our

house ."

"Yes, Mama ," said Epaminondas.

"I won't forget."

sun

May

dog

Mama

The next day, as soon as the  came up, Epaminondas again ran to visit his Auntie . This time, when he was ready to leave, she gave him a  . Epaminondas was very happy. But he remembered what his had told him.

So he wrapped the  in some  and stopped now and then to cool it in the  as he hurried along the  to his  .

For he was a good little  and he always did EXACTLY as he was told.

leaves

river

road

house

boy

dog

Mama

But by the time Epaminondas

got home, the  was very wet!

"Oh, dear," said his . "That

is no way to carry a ! Next

time find a piece of  and tie

it around his neck. Then lead him

along the 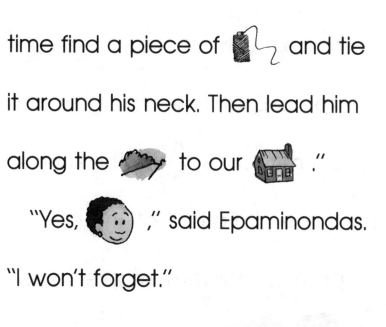 to our  ."

"Yes,  ," said Epaminondas.

"I won't forget."

string

road

house

sun

May

bread

Mama

string

The next day, as soon as the came up, Epaminondas again ran to see his Auntie . This time she gave him a loaf of .

Epaminondas remembered what his had told him. So he found a piece of and tied it to the

road

house

boy

 . Then he dragged the

down the  to his  .

For he was a good little  and

he always did EXACTLY as he was told.

But when Epaminondas got

home the  was too dirty to eat.

Mama

steps

five

pies

"Oh, no!" said his  . "You had better sit on these and be good while I go make supper. And I don't want to see you step in those apple I set out to cool."

So Epaminondas waited until his went inside—so she WOULD NOT see him step in those !

But those  looked awfully good. Did his really want him to step in them?

Epaminondas decided to wait and ask. Why ruin 5 delicious apple if he didn't have to! What do you think?

Words I can read

☐ boy
☐ bread
☐ butter
☐ cake
☐ crumbs
☐ dog
☐ five
☐ hands

☐ hat
☐ house
☐ leaves
☐ Mama
☐ May
☐ pies
☐ river
☐ road

☐ steps
☐ string
☐ sun